Paul
Jennings

Three Quirky Tails

PENGUIN BOOKS

PENGUIN BOOKS

Published by the Penguin Group
Penguin Books Ltd, 27 Wrights Lane, London w8 5TZ, England
Penguin Books USA Inc., 375 Hudson Street, New York, New York 10014, USA
Penguin Books Australia Ltd, Ringwood, Victoria, Australia
Penguin Books Canada Ltd, 10 Alcorn Avenue, Toronto, Ontario, Canada M4V 3B2
Penguin Books (NZ) Ltd, 182–190 Wairau Road, Auckland 10, New Zealand

Penguin Books Ltd, Registered Offices: Harmondsworth, Middlesex, England

First published in *Quirky Tails* by Penguin Books Australia 1987
Published in Great Britain in Puffin Books 1992

This collection published in Penguin Books 1996
1 3 5 7 9 10 8 6 4 2

Set in 12/15pt Monophoto Bembo
Typeset by Datix International Limited, Bungay, Suffolk
Printed in England by Clays Ltd, St Ives plc

Contents

Tonsil Eye 'Tis

GOOD grief. I am gone. I have had it. That good looking girl from next door has seen me pulling the hairs out of my nose. She thinks I am grotty. Now I will have to tell her the whole story because I can see by the look on her face that she is disgusted. I have already lost Tara, my girlfriend. I couldn't stand it if Jill gets the wrong idea too.

'Listen, Jill. Don't look like that. There is a very good reason why I do it. You don't think I like pulling the hairs out of my nose do you? It is very painful.'

Jill is not saying anything. She is just staring at me so I go on with the story. 'This little garden gnome business is only here because of my nose-hair pulling. You don't believe me? Well look at this.'

I take my hand off the new garden gnome's head and show her the eye that has grown on the end of my finger. I have never shown anyone this little eye before. I can see with it, which is a fairly unusual thing. When I am not making gnomes I keep a glove on so that no one can see the eye. Jill's mouth is hanging open with surprise so I decide to tell her about the way the whole thing happened before she thinks I have gone crazy.

It all begins when my girlfriend Tara gives me a garden gnome for my fourteenth birthday. It is a horrible looking garden gnome and it only has one eye. 'It's lovely,' I say to Tara. 'Just what I wanted. A little angry looking garden gnome.'

It is angry looking, too. Its one and only eye glares at everyone as if its toenails are being pulled out. And its mouth is wide open like someone yelling out swear words at the footy. It is made out of cement but it is very realistic.

'I am so glad you like it,' says Tara in a dangerous voice. 'Because it cost me a lot of money.'

'I can see that,' I answer. 'Anyone can tell that it is a very special garden gnome. I know just the spot for it – down behind the garden shed.'

'Behind the garden shed,' yells Tara. 'You can't put it out in the rain. I don't think you like it.'

'I was only joking,' I say quickly. 'I will put it on the shelf where I can see it all the time.'

So that is how the garden gnome comes to be in my

bedroom. Every morning and every night there it is glaring at me. As the days go by it seems to look grumpier and grumpier.

After a while I find that I can't sleep at night. The angry gnome gets into my dreams. I wake up at night and find that I can't stop staring at its horrible little face. I keep having a nightmare about being swallowed by it.

I turn the gnome around so that it faces the wall but this does not work either. I keep imagining that it is pulling faces. Finally I can stand it no more. I grab the gnome by its silly little red hat and am just about to smash it to smithereens when I notice something strange. Inside its mouth, right at the back, is a tiny little face about half the size of a pea. It is stuck on the gnome's tonsils.

I think that whoever made this garden gnome has a strange sense of humour. I decide to remove the little face from the gnome's tonsils. I get a small hammer and a screwdriver and I start chipping away at the little face at the back of the gnome's throat. I feel a bit like a dentist. The gnome's mouth is wide open but I bet he would close it if he could.

After a couple of hits the little face flies off the gnome's tonsils and falls on to its tongue.

The next bit is hard to believe but it really does happen. The little round face rolls along the garden gnome's concrete tongue, on to its lips and flies through the air. It hits me full in the mouth. 'Ouch,' I yell at the top of my voice. 'That hurt.'

It is so painful that my eyes start to water. I am really mad now and I start searching around on the carpet for the little round face. It is nowhere to be seen. I search and search but I can't find it anywhere. My lips are still hurting and I have a funny, tickling feeling somewhere at the back of my throat.

'Right,' I yell at the gnome. 'You have had it.' I pick up the screwdriver and throw it as hard as I can. The point of the screwdriver hits the gnome on his one and only eye and knocks it clean out of his face. Now the gnome has no eyes at all. It is lucky it is only made out of concrete or it would be a very unhappy gnome.

I look around the floor for the eye but I can't find that either. This is when I notice that one of my fingers on my right hand is feeling sore.

What happens next is really weird. I find myself looking up at my own face. It is just as if I am lying on the carpet looking up at myself. I am looking down and up at the same time. My head starts to swim. I feel I must be having a nightmare. I hope I am having a nightmare because if not I must be going nuts. There on the end of one of my fingers, is a little eye. A real eye. It is staring and blinking and I can see with it.

The gnome's eye has somehow grown on to my finger.

I give a scream of rage and fear and then I grab the gnome and run outside with it. I throw it down on to the path and smash it to pieces with the hammer. By the time I am finished all that is left is a small pile of dust and powder.

The gnome is gone for good but the eye is not. No, the eye is still there, blinking and winking on the end of my finger. I shove my hand in my pocket because I can't bear to look at my extra eye. Suddenly I can see what is in my pocket. There is a used tissue, two cents (which is all the money I have in the world) and a half-sucked licorice block. The eye is looking around inside my pocket.

I grin. At first I think that maybe this is not too bad. An extra eye on the end of a finger might be useful. I go back to my bedroom and poke my finger into a little hole in the wall. There is a family of mice nesting there. They get a big fright when they see the finger-eye looking at them and they nick off as fast as they can go.

Next I stick my finger into my earhole to see what is going on in there. My new eye seems to be able to see in the dark, but to be quite honest, there is not really much action inside an ear.

This is when I get the idea to have a peek inside my own mouth. I have always wondered what it is like at the back of my throat and this is my big chance to find out. I poke my finger in and have a look around. It is quite interesting really, I have never seen behind that thing that dangles down at the back before. There are a lot of red, wet mountains back there.

Suddenly I see something terrible. Horrible. A little face is staring back at me. It is the little round face that I chipped off the gnome's tonsils. It has taken up residence in my throat. It lives behind my tonsils.

I start to cough and splutter. I have to get it out.

Fancy having a little round face living in your throat. I try everything I can think of to get it out (including blowing my nose about a thousand times) but it just will not come out.

'Okay,' I say. 'If you will not come out by force I will get you out with brains.' I go down to the kitchen to see what there is to eat. I notice a packet of Hundreds and Thousands that Mum uses to sprinkle on top of cakes.

'Just the right size,' I say to myself. I put three of the Hundreds and Thousands on my tongue and put my finger up to my mouth to see what happens. Sure enough, the little face rolls on to my tongue and eats two of them. It eats the red ones but doesn't seem to like the blue one.

'Right,' I say. I pick out about fifteen red Hundreds and Thousands and put them on my tongue so that they form a little trail. The trail leads on to my lip and down my chin. I open my mouth and watch with the eye on my finger from a distance. The little face rolls out and starts eating. He reaches my lips and still he is not suspicious. A bit later he looks around outside and then moves down to my chin to eat the Hundreds and Thousands I have put there.

As quick as a flash I close my mouth and leave him trapped on the outside. I have won. Or so I think.

The little face tries to burrow back through my closed lips but I have my teeth clenched together. He can't get in.

I raise my hand to grab him, but before I can, he races upwards and disappears into my nose. In about two seconds I can feel him back behind my tonsils. I know that he will not fall for the Hundreds and Thousands trick again.

Just then, there is a knock at the front door. I walk down the hall and put my finger up to the keyhole to see who it is. It is Tara, my girlfriend. I open the door and give her a weak smile. 'G'day,' I say. 'How are you doing?'

'I have come to have a look at the garden gnome I gave you,' she says. 'I want to make sure that you haven't put it down the back yard.'

My heart sinks. Tara is standing next to a pile of powder and dust that is the remains of the gnome. She has not seen it yet.

'Come in and sit down,' I say. I try to think of an
explanation but I know that I can't tell Tara. She

won't like the little face on my tonsils. She certainly won't like my extra eye. Once she wouldn't go out with me just because I had a pimple on my ear. If I tell her the truth she will drop me like a brick.

I can feel the little face moving around at the back of my throat. I have to know what he is up to so I put my finger into my mouth to see what is going on.

'What are you sucking your finger for?' asks Tara.

The little face is right on the end of the dangler thing in my throat. He is swinging on it having fun.

'Take your finger out of your mouth and answer me, you silly boy,' Tara snaps.

The little face is hanging on to the dangler by his teeth! It hurts like nothing.

'Stop sucking your finger, you idiot,' yells Tara.

Now the face is out of sight. He is hiding up the back somewhere. I shove my finger in further to find out what is going on. This is a big mistake. I touch something that I shouldn't with my finger and it makes me sick. I spew up all over the carpet. Some of it splashes on Tara's shoes.

I get down on to my hands and knees and start sifting through the spew. I hope that the little face has been swept out with the tide. But it hasn't.

'You revolting creep,' yells Tara. 'I am breaking it off. You're dropped. I never want to see you again in my life.' She stands up and charges out of the door.

'Good riddance,' I yell. 'And take your rotten gnome with you. You will find what is left of it on the footpath.'

I stagger out into the front garden and sit down. I feel terrible. My life is ruined. My girlfriend has dropped me. I have no money (except for two cents). I have an eye on my finger and a little face in my throat. I wish I was dead. I start to cry. Tears fall down my face. And down my finger. The eye on my finger is shedding tears too. Little teardrops fall on to the grass.

Then something amazing starts to happen. Where the tears from my finger are falling, little concrete gnomes start to grow in the grass. I can't believe it. They are sad little gnomes but they are very life-like. They look just as if they are alive.

Ten little gnomes grow, one for each teardrop. The next day I sell the gnomes for ten dollars each. I make a hundred dollars profit.

Jill is listening to my story with wide open eyes. I don't suppose she will believe it.

'Well,' says Jill. 'What a sad tale.'

'Yes,' I answer. I can hardly believe my ears. Jill believes the whole thing. This is when I notice what a spunk she really is.

'What I can't understand,' she goes on. 'Is what all this had to do with pulling hairs out of your nose.'

I feel a bit embarrassed but I decide to tell her the truth. 'I am trying to grow more gnomes,' I say. 'But I can't make any tears come. When you pull the hairs in your nose it makes your eyes water.' I hold up my finger and show her my extra eye again.

'Is the little face still there?' she asks.

'Yes.'

'And have you got any more Hundreds and Thousands?'

'Yes,' I answer again, handing over the packet.

'Well,' she says. 'We can't have you pulling hairs out of your nose. It's not a nice habit. Open up your mouth and let me speak to the face.'

I open my mouth and Jill looks inside and speaks to my guest. 'Listen,' she says. 'We don't mind you living in there. But fair's fair. You have to pay the rent. You help us and we will help you.'

So this is how Jill becomes my girlfriend. And we both become very rich from selling garden gnomes. We have got the perfect system. I open up my mouth and Jill calls out instructions to my tenant.

The little face goes up and pulls on a hair in my nose with his teeth. This makes my eye water and drop tears on to the lawn. More concrete gnomes grow out of the grass. Then we give the face his reward – red Hundreds and Thousands.

The gnomes are so realistic that we get five hundred dollars each for them. This means I don't have to have my hairs pulled very often.

You don't believe the story? Well, all I can say is this. If you are ever thinking of buying a garden gnome have a look in its mouth first. If there is a little face on its tonsils – don't buy it.

The Copy

I WAS rapt. It was the best day of my life. I had asked Fiona to go with me and she said yes. I couldn't believe it. I mean it wasn't as if I was a great catch. I was skinny, weak, and not too smart at school. Mostly I got Cs and Ds for marks. And I couldn't play sport at all. I hated football, always went out on the first ball at cricket and didn't know which end to hold a tennis racquet. And Fiona had still said she'd be my girlfriend.

Every boy in year eleven at Hamilton High would be jealous. Especially Mat Hodson. It was no secret that he fancied Fiona too. I grinned to myself. I wished I could see his face when he found out the news. He thought that he was so great and in a way he was. He was the exact opposite to me. He was smart (always got As for everything), captain of the footy team, the best batsman in the cricket team and he was tough. Real tough. He could flatten me with one punch if he wanted to. I just hoped he took it with good grace about Fiona and me. I didn't want him for an enemy.

I headed off to Crankshaft Alley to see my old friend Dr Woolley. I always went to see him when something good happened. Or something bad. I felt sort of safe and happy inside his untidy old workshop and it was fun seeing what crazy thing he was inventing. Everything he had come up with so far had been a flop. His last invention was warm clothespegs to stop people getting cold fingers when they hung out the clothes. They worked all right but no one would buy them because they cost two hundred dollars each. All of his inventions had turned out like that. They worked and they were clever but they were too expensive for people to buy.

I walked on down past all the other little shop-front factories until I reached Dr Woolley's grubby door. I gave the secret knock (three slow, three fast) and his gnomish face appeared at the window. I say gnomish because he looked just like a gnome: he was short with a hooked nose and he had a white beard and a bald head surrounded with a ring of white hair. If you gave him a fishing rod and a red cap and sat him in the front yard you would think he was a little garden statue.

He opened the door. 'Come in Rodney,' he said.

'Tim,' I corrected. He always called me the wrong name. He had a terrible memory.

'Where's that screwdriver?' he said. 'It's always getting lost.'

'In your hand,' I told him.

'Thanks, Peter, thanks.'

'Tim,' I sighed. I don't know why I bothered. He was never going to call me by my right name. It wasn't that he didn't know who I was. He did. I was his only friend. Everyone else thought he was a dangerous crackpot because he chased them away from his front door with a broken mop. I was the only person allowed into his workshop.

'Are you still working on the Cloner?' I asked.

His face turned grim and he furtively looked over at the window. 'Sh . . . Not so loud. Someone might hear. I've almost perfected it. I'm nearly there. And this time it is going to pay off.' He led me across the room to a machine that looked something like a telephone box with a whole lot of wires hanging out of it. Down one side were a number of dials and switches. There were two red buttons. One was labelled COPY and the other REVERSE.

Dr Woolley placed a pinecone on the floor of the Cloner. Then he pressed the button that said COPY. There was a whirring sound and a puff of smoke and then, amazingly, the outline of another pinecone, exactly the same as the first, appeared. It lasted for about ten seconds and then the machine started to rock and shake and the whirring slowly died. The image of the second pinecone faded away.

'Fantastic,' I yelled.

'Blast,' said Dr Woolley. 'It's unstable. It won't hold the copy. But I'm nearly there. I think I know how to fix it.'

'What will you use it for?' I asked. 'What's the good of copying pinecones? There are plenty of pinecones already. We don't need more of those.'

He started to get excited. 'Listen, Robert.'

'Tim,' I said.

'Tim, then. It doesn't only work with pinecones. It will work with anything.' He looked up at the window as he said it. Then he dropped his voice. 'What if I made a copy of a bar of gold, eh? What then? And then another copy and another and another. We would be rich. Rich.'

16

I started to get excited too. I liked the way he said 'we'.

Dr Woolley started nodding his little head up and down. 'All I need is time,' he said. 'Time to get the adjustment right. Then we will show them whether I'm a crank or not.'

We had a cup of tea together and then I headed off home. That was two good things that had happened in one day. First, Fiona saying she would go with me and second, the Cloner was nearly working. I whistled all the way home.

I didn't see Dr Woolley for some time after that. I had a lot on my mind. I had to walk home with Fiona and every night I went to her place to study with her. Not that we got much study done. On weekends we went hiking or hung around listening to records. It was the best time of my life. There was only one blot on the horizon. Mat Hodson. One of his mates had told me he was out to get me. He left a message saying he was going to flatten me for taking his girl.

His girl! Fiona couldn't stand him. She told me she thought he was a show off and a bully. But that wasn't going to help me. If he wanted to flatten me he would get me in the end. Fortunately he had caught the mumps and had to stay at home for three weeks. Someone had told me it was very painful.

I decided to go round to see Dr Woolley about a month later. I wondered if he had perfected his Cloner. When I reached the door I gave the secret knock but there was no answer. 'That's strange,' I said to myself. 'He never goes out for anything.'

I looked through the window and although the curtains were drawn I could see the light was on inside. I knocked again on the door but still no answer. Then I started to worry. What if he had had a heart attack or something? He could be lying unconscious on the floor. I ran around to the back, got the key from the hiding spot in an old kettle and let myself into the workshop. The place was in a mess. Tables and chairs were turned over and crockery was lying smashed on the floor. It looked as if there had been a fight in the workshop. There was no sign of Dr Woolley.

I started to clean the place up, turning the chairs up the right way and putting the broken things into the bin. That's when I found the letter. It was in an envelope marked with four names. It said, 'John', 'Peter',

'Robert', and 'Tim'. The first three names were crossed out. Dr Woolley had finally remembered my name was Tim after four tries. Inside the letter said:

TIM

IF YOU FIND THIS LETTER SOMETHING TERRIBLE
HAS HAPPENED. YOU MUST DESTROY THE
CLONER AT ONCE.

WOOLLEY

My eye caught something else on the floor. I went over and picked it up. It was another letter exactly the same as the first. Exactly the same. It even had the three wrong names crossed out. Dr Woolley really was the most absent-minded person.

I looked at the Cloner with a feeling of dread. What had happened? Why did he want me to destroy it? And where was Dr Woolley? The Cloner was switched on. I could tell that because the red light next to REVERSE was shining. I walked over to it and switched it over to COPY. I don't know what made me do it. I guess I just wanted to know if the Cloner worked. I should have left it alone but I didn't. I took a Biro out of my top pocket and threw it inside the Cloner.

Immediately an image of another Biro formed. There were two of them where before there had only been one. I turned the Cloner off and picked up both pens. As far as I could tell they were identical. I couldn't tell which was the real one. They were both real.

I sat down on a chair feeling a bit dizzy. This was the most fantastic machine that had ever been invented. It could make me rich. Dr Woolley had said that it could even copy gold bars. All sorts of wonderful ideas came into my mind. I decided that nothing would make me destroy the Cloner.

I went over and switched the machine on to RE-VERSE. Then I threw both of the pens into the Cloner. I was shocked by what happened. Both of them disappeared. They were gone. For good. I turned it back to COPY but nothing happened. I tried REVERSE again but still nothing. It was then that I noticed a huge blowfly buzzing around the room. It flew crazily around my head and then headed straight into the Cloner. It vanished without a trace.

The Cloner was dangerous when it was switched on to REVERSE. It could make things vanish for good. I wondered if Dr Woolley had fallen into the machine.

Or had he been pushed? There were certainly signs of a struggle.

I thought about going to the Police. But what could they do? They couldn't help Dr Woolley if he had fallen into the Cloner. And they would take it away and I would never see it again. I didn't want that to happen. I had plans for that machine. It was mine now. I was the rightful owner. After all, Dr Woolley had said that 'we' would be rich. Unfortunately now it was just going to be me who was rich.

I went back to Fiona's house and spent the evening doing homework with her. I didn't tell her about the Cloner. I was going to give her the first copies I made from it. At ten o'clock I walked home through the darkened streets, keeping an eye out for Mat Hodson. I had heard he was over his mumps and was looking for me.

The next morning I borrowed Mum's gold cameo brooch without telling her. I decided not to go to school but instead I went to Dr Woolley's workshop. Once inside I turned the Cloner on to COPY and threw in the brooch. Immediately another one appeared. I turned the Cloner off and took out both brooches.

One was a mirror image of the other. They both had the same gold setting and the same ivory face. But on one brooch the face looked to the left and on the other it looked to the right. Apart from that they were identical.

I whistled to myself. The copy was so good I couldn't remember which way Mum's brooch had faced. Still it didn't matter. I would put one of them back where I had got it and give the other to Fiona.

Next I decided to experiment with something that was alive. I went outside and hunted around in the long grass. After a while I found a small green frog with a black patch on its left side. I took it in and threw it straight into the Cloner. In a flash there were two frogs. They jumped out onto the workshop floor. I picked them up and looked at them. They were both alive and perfectly happy. They were both green but one had a black patch on the left and the other had it on the right. One was a mirror image of the other.

This Cloner was wonderful. I spent all day there making copies of everything I could think of. By four o'clock there was two of almost everything in the workshop. I decided it was time to go and give Fiona her cameo. She was going to be very happy to get it.

I never made it to Fiona's house. An unpleasant surprise was waiting outside for me. It was Mat Hodson.

'I've been waiting for you, you little fink,' he said. 'I heard you were hiding in here.' He had a pair of footy boots hanging around his neck. He was on his way to practice. He gave a nasty leer. 'I thought I told you to stay away from my girl.'

'She's not your girl,' I said hotly. 'She can't stand you. She's my . . .' I never finished the sentence. He hit me with a tremendous punch in the guts and I went down like an exploding balloon. The pain was terrible and I couldn't breathe. I fought for air but nothing happened. I was winded. And all I could do was lay there on the footpath wriggling like a dying worm.

'You get one of those every day,' he said. 'Until you break it off with Fiona.' Then he laughed and went off to footy practice.

After a while my breath started to come back in great sobs and spasms. I staggered back into the workshop and sat down. I was mad. I was out of my mind. I had to think of some way to stop him. I couldn't go through this every day and I couldn't give up Fiona. I needed help. And badly. But I couldn't think of anyone. I didn't have a friend who would help me fight Hodson except Fiona and I couldn't ask her.

My mind was in a whirl and my stomach ached like crazy. I wasn't thinking straight. That's why I did the stupidest thing of my life. I decided to get inside the Cloner and turn it on. There would be two of me. Two Tims. I could get The Copy to help me fight Hodson. He would help me. After all, he would be the same as me. He would want to pay Hodson back as much as I did. The more I thought about it, the smarter it seemed.

I would make an exact copy of myself and together we could go off and flatten Hodson. I wondered what my first words to the new arrival should be. In the end I decided to say, 'Hello there, welcome to earth.' I know it sounds corny but at the time it was all I could think of.

I turned the Cloner to COPY and jumped in before I lost my nerve. In a twinkling there was another 'me' standing there. It was just like looking into a mirror.

He had the same jeans, the same jumper and the same

brown eyes. We both stood staring at each other for about thirty seconds without saying a thing. Then, both at the same time we said, 'Hello, there, welcome to earth.'

That gave me a heck of a shock. How did he know what I was going to say? I couldn't figure it out. It wasn't until much later I realized he knew all about me. He had an exact copy of my brain. He knew everything I had ever done. He knew what I had been thinking before I stepped into the Cloner. That's why he was able to say the same sentence. He knew everything about me. He even knew how many times I had kissed Fiona. The Copy wasn't just a copy. He was me.

We both stood there again for about thirty seconds with our brains ticking over. We were both trying to make sense of the situation. I drew a breath to say something but he beat me to it. 'Well,' he said. 'What are we waiting for? Let's go get Hodson.'

The Copy and I jogged along the street towards the football ground without speaking. I wondered what he was thinking. He didn't know what I was thinking. We shared the same past but not the same future or present. From now on everything that happened would be experienced differently by both of us. I didn't have the faintest idea what was going on in his head. But I knew what was going on in mine. I was wondering how I was going to get rid of him when this was all over.

'Fiona will like that brooch,' said The Copy. I was shocked to think he knew about it. He was smiling to himself. I went red. He was probably thinking Fiona was going to give him a nice big kiss when she saw that brooch. It was me she was going to kiss, not The Copy.

At last we reached the football ground. Hodson was just coming out of the changing rooms. 'Well look,' he said. 'It's little Tim and his twin brother. Brought him to help you, have you?' he said to The Copy. 'Well, I can handle both of you.' He screwed up his hand into a tight fist. Suddenly he looked very big. In fact he looked big enough to wipe the floor with both of us.

I felt like running for it. So did The Copy. I could see he was just about to turn around and run off, leaving me on my own. We both turned and fled.

Hodson chased after us for a bit and finally gave it away. 'See you tomorrow, boys,' he yelled. I could hear the other footballers laughing at us. It was humiliating. I knew the others would tell Fiona about what a coward I was.

I turned to The Copy. 'A fat lot of use you turned out to be,' I said.

'What are you talking about,' he replied. 'You're the one who turned and ran off first. You knew I couldn't handle him on my own.'

I realized The Copy was a liar. I decided to go home for tea. He walked along beside me. 'Where do you think you're going?' I asked.

'Home for tea.'

'We can't both turn up for tea. What's Mum going to say when she sees two of us? The shock will kill her,' I told him.

We both kept on walking towards home. The Copy knew the way. He knew everything I knew. Except what I was thinking. He only knew about what had happened before he came out of the Cloner. He didn't know what was going on in my mind after that. I stopped. He seemed determined to come home with 27 me. 'Look,' I said. 'Be reasonable. Think of Mum and Dad. We can't both sit down for tea. You go somewhere else.'

'No,' he said. 'You go somewhere else.'

Finally we came to the front gate. 'All right,' I said to The Copy. 'You go and hide in the bedroom. I'll go down to tea and afterwards I'll sneak you up some food.'

The Copy didn't like it. 'I've got a better idea,' he told me. 'You hide in the bedroom and I'll bring you up something.'

I could see he was only thinking of himself. This thing was turning into a nightmare. 'All right,' I said in the end. 'You go down to tea and I'll hide in the bedroom.' So that is what we did. I sneaked up and hid in my room while The Copy had tea with my parents. It was roast pork. My favourite. I could smell it from my room and it smelt delicious.

The sound of laughter and chattering floated up the stairs. No one knew The Copy wasn't me. They couldn't tell the difference. A bit later he came up the stairs. He poked his head around the corner and threw me a couple of dry biscuits. 'This is all I could find. I'll try and bring you up something later.'

Dry biscuits. I had to eat dry biscuits while The Copy finished off my tea. And I just remembered Mum had been cooking apple pie before we left. This was too much. Something had to be done.

Just then the doorbell rang. 'I'll get it,' shouted The Copy before I had a chance to open my mouth. He ran down the stairs and answered the door. I was trapped. I couldn't go down or Mum and Dad would see there were two of us.

I could hear a girl's voice. It was Fiona. A bit later the door closed and all was silent. The Copy had gone outside with her. I raced over to the window and looked out. It was dark but I could just see them under the wattle tree. The street light illuminated the scene. What I saw made my blood boil. The Copy was kissing Fiona. He was kissing my girlfriend. She thought he was me. She couldn't tell the difference and she was letting the creep kiss her. And what is worse she seemed to be enjoying it. It was a very long kiss.

I sat down and thought about the situation. The Copy had to be sent back to where he came from. This whole thing had turned out to be a terrible mistake. I had to get The Copy back to the workshop and get rid of him.

After about two hours The Copy came up to the bedroom looking very pleased with himself. I bit my tongue and didn't say anything about him kissing Fiona. 'Look,' I said. 'We can't both stay here. Why don't we go back to the workshop and have a good talk. Then we can figure out what to do.'

He thought about it for a bit and then he said. 'Okay, you're right. We had better work something out.'

I snuck out of the window and met him outside. We walked all the way to the workshop in silence. I could tell he didn't like me any more than I liked him.

I took the key out of the kettle and let us in. I noticed the Cloner was still switched on to COPY. I went over and turned it on to REVERSE without saying anything. It would all be over quickly. He wouldn't know what hit him. I would just push him straight into the Cloner and everything would be back to normal. He would be gone and there would be just me. It wouldn't be murder. I mean he had only been alive for a few hours and he wasn't really a person. He was just a copy.

'Look,' I said, pointing to the floor of the Cloner. 'Look at this,' I got ready to push him straight in when he came over.

The Copy came over for a look. Suddenly he grabbed me and started to push me towards the machine. The Copy was trying to kill me. He was trying to push me into the Cloner and have Fiona for himself. We fell to the floor in a struggling heap. It was a terrible fight. We both had exactly the same strength and the same experience. As we fought I realized what had happened to Dr Woolley. He had made a copy of himself and they had both tried to push each other in. That's why there were two letters. Probably they had both fallen in and killed each other.

The Copy and I fought for about ten minutes. Neither of us could get the upper hand and we were both growing tired. We rolled over near the bench and I noticed an iron bar on the floor. But The Copy had noticed it too. We both tried to reach it at the same time. But I won. I grabbed it and wrenched my arm free. With a great whack I crashed it down over The Copy's head. He fell to the floor in a heap.

I dragged his lifeless body over to the Cloner and shoved him inside. He vanished without a trace. It was just as if he had never existed. A feeling of great relief spread over me but I was shaking at the narrow escape I had experienced. I turned and ran home without even locking up the workshop.

By the time I got home I felt a lot better. I walked into the lounge where Mum and Dad were sitting watching TV. Dad looked up at me. 'Ah there you are, Tim. Would you fill out this application for the school camp? You put in the details and I'll sign the bottom.'

I took the form and started to fill it in. I was looking forward to the school camp. We were going skiing. After a while I looked up. Mum and Dad were both staring at me in a funny way.

'What's up?' I asked.

'You're writing with your left hand,' said Dad.

'So?'

'You've been a right hander all your life.'

'And your hair is parted on the wrong side,' said Mum. 'And that little mole that used to be on your right cheek has moved to the left side.'

My head started to swim. I ran over to the mirror on the wall. The face that stared back at me was not Tim's. It was the face of The Copy.

No Is Yes

THE question is: did the girl kill her own father? Some say yes and some say no.

Linda doesn't look like a murderess.

She walks calmly up the steps of the high school stage. She shakes the mayor's hand and receives her award. Top of the school. She moves over to the microphone to make her speech of acceptance. She is seventeen, beautiful and in love. Her words are delicate, musical crystals falling upon receptive ears. The crowd rewards her clarity with loud applause but it passes her by. She is seeking a face among the visitors in the front row. She finds what she is looking for and her eyes meet those of a young man. They both smile.

He knows the answer.

'It's finally finished,' said Dr Scrape. 'After fourteen years of research it is finished.' He tapped the thick manuscript on the table. 'And you, Ralph, will be the first to see the results.'

They were sitting in the lounge watching the sun lower itself once more into the grave of another day.

Ralph didn't seem quite sure what to say. He was unsure of himself. In the end he came out with. 'Fourteen years is a lot of work. What's it all about?'

Dr Scrape stroked his pointed little beard and leaned across the coffee table. 'Tell me,' he said, 'As a layman, how did you learn to speak? How did you learn the words and grammar of the English language?'

'Give us a go,' said Ralph good naturedly. 'I haven't had an education like you. I haven't been to university. I didn't even finish high school. I don't know about stuff like that. You're the one with all the brains. You tell me. How did I learn to speak?'

When Ralph said, 'You're the one with all the brains,' Dr Scrape smiled to himself and nodded wisely. 'Have a guess then,' he insisted.

'Me mother. Me mother taught me to talk.'

'No.'

'Me father then.'

'No.'

.'Then who?' asked Ralph with a tinge of annoyance.

'Nobody taught you,' exclaimed Dr Scrape. 'Nobody teaches children to talk. They just learn it by listening. If the baby is in China it will learn Chinese because that's what it hears. If you get a new-born Chinese baby and bring it here it will learn to speak English not Chinese. Just by listening to those around it.'

'What's that got to do with your re . . .?' began Ralph. But he stopped. Dr Scrape's daughter entered the room with a tray. She was a delicate, pale girl of about fourteen. Her face reminded Ralph of a porcelain doll. He was struck by both her beauty and her shyness.

'This is my daughter, Linda,' said Dr Scrape with a flourish.

'G'day,' said Ralph awkwardly.

'And this is Mr Pickering.'

She made no reply at first but simply stood there staring at him as if he were a creature from another planet. He felt like some exotic animal in the zoo which was of total fascination to someone on the other side of the bars.

Dr Scrape frowned and the girl suddenly remembered her manners.

'How do you do?' she said awkwardly. 'Would you like some coffee?'

'Thanks a lot,' said Ralph.

'White or black?'

'Black, thanks.'

Linda raised an eyebrow at her father. 'The usual for me,' he said with a smirk. Ralph Pickering watched as Linda poured two cups of tea and put milk into both of them. She looked up, smiled and handed him one of the cups.

'Thanks a lot,' he said again.

'Salt?' she asked, proferring a bowl filled with white crystals.

Ralph looked at the bowl with a red face. He felt uncomfortable in this elegant house. He didn't know the right way to act. He didn't have the right manners. He didn't know why he had been asked in for a cup of coffee. He was just the apprentice plumber here to fix the drains. He looked down at his grubby overalls and mud encrusted shoes.

'Er, eh?' said Ralph.

'Salt?' she asked again holding out the bowl.

Ralph shook his head with embarrassment. Did they

really have salt in their tea? He sipped from the delicate china cup. He liked coffee, black and with sugar, in a nice big mug. Somehow he had ended up with white tea, no sugar and a fragile cup which rattled in his big hands.

He had the feeling, though, that Linda had not meant to embarrass him. If there was any malevolence it came from Dr Scrape who was grinning hugely at Ralph's discomfort.

Ralph Pickering scratched his head with his broken fingernails.

The young girl looked at her watch. 'Will you be staying for breakfast?' she asked Ralph kindly. 'We are having roast pork. It's nearly washed.'

'N, n, no thanks,' he stumbled. 'My mum is expecting me home for tea. I couldn't stay the night.' He noticed a puzzled expression on her face and she shook her head as if not quite understanding him. The oddest feeling came over him that she thought he was a bit mad.

Ralph moved as if to stand up.

'Don't go yet,' said Dr Scrape. 'I haven't finished telling you about my research. Although you have already seen some of it.' He nodded towards his daughter who had gone into the kitchen and could be heard preparing the pork for the evening meal. 'Now where were we?' he went on. 'Ah yes. About learning to speak. So you see, my dear boy, we learn to speak just from hearing those around us talking.' He was waving his hands around as if delivering a lecture to a large audience. His eyes lit up with excitement. 'But ask yourself this. What if a child was born and never heard anyone speak except on the television? Never ever saw a real human being, only the television? Would the television do just as well as live people? Could they learn to talk then?'

He paused, not really expecting Ralph to say anything. Then he answered his own question. 'No one knows,' he exclaimed thrusting a finger into the air. 'It's never been done.'

'It would be cruel,' said Ralph, suddenly forgetting his shyness. 'You couldn't bring up a child who had never heard anyone speak. It'd be a dirty trick. That's why it's never been done.'

'Right,' yelled Dr Scrape. His little beard was waggling away as he spoke. 'So I did the next best thing. I never let her hear anybody speak except me.' He nodded towards the kitchen.

'You mean . . .' began Ralph.

'Yes, yes. Linda. My daughter. She has never heard anyone in the world speak except me. You are the first person apart from me she has ever spoken to.'

'You mean she has never been to school?'

'No.'

'Or kindergarten?'

'No.'

'Or shopping or to the beach?'

'No, she's never been out of this house.'

'But why?' asked Ralph angrily. 'What for?'

'It's an experiment, boy. She has learned a lot of words incorrectly. Just by listening to me use the wrong words. All without a single lesson. I call "up" "down" and "down" "up". I call "sugar" "salt". "Yes" is "no" and "no" is "yes". It's been going on ever since she was a baby. I have taught her thousands of words incorrectly. She thinks that room in there is called the laundry,' he yelled pointing to the kitchen. 'I have let her watch television every day and all day but it makes no difference. She can't get it right.'

He picked up a spoon and chuckled. 'She calls this a carpet. And this,' he said holding up a fork, 'she calls a chicken. Even when she sees a chicken on television she doesn't wake up. She doesn't change. She doesn't notice it. It proves my hypothesis: point that is,' he added for the benefit of Ralph whom he considered to be an idiot. 'So you see, I have made a big break-through. I have proved that humans can't learn to speak properly from listening to television. Real people are needed.'

'You know something,' said Ralph slowly. 'If this is true, if you have really taught the poor kid all the wrong words . . .'

Dr Scrape interrupted. 'Of course it's true. Of course it's true.' He took out a worn exercise book and flipped over the pages. 'Here they are. Over two thousand words – all learned incorrectly. Usually the opposites. Whenever I talk with Linda I use these words. She doesn't know the difference. Dog is cat, tree is lamp post, ant is elephant and just for fun girl is boy – she calls herself a boy although of course she knows she is the opposite sex to you. She would call you a girl.' He gave a low, devilish laugh.

Ralph's anger had completely swamped his shyness and his feeling of awkwardness caused by the splendour of the mansion. 'You are a dirty mongrel,' he said quietly. 'The poor thing has never met another person but you – and what a low specimen you are. And you've mixed her all up. How is she going to get on in the real world?'

'You mean in on the real world, not on in the real world,' he smirked. Then he began to laugh. He thought it was a great joke. 'You'll have to get used to it,' he said. 'When you talk to her you'll have to get used to everything being back to front.'

'What's it got to do with me?'

'Why, I want you to try her out. Talk to her. See how she goes. Before I give my paper and show her to the world I want to make sure that it lasts. That she won't break down and start speaking correctly with strangers. I want you to be the first test. I want a common working man . . . boy,' he corrected. 'One who can't pull any linguistic tricks.'

'Leave me out of it,' said Ralph forcefully. 'I don't want any part of it. It's cruel and, and,' he searched around for a word. 'Rotten,' he spat out.

Scrape grabbed his arm and spun him round. He was dribbling with false sincerity. 'But if you really care, if you really care about her you will try to help. Go on,' he said pushing Ralph towards the kitchen. 'Tell her what a despicable creature I am. Tell her the difference between salt and sugar. Set her straight. That's the least you can do. Or don't you care at all?' He narrowed his eyes.

Ralph pushed him off and strode towards the kitchen. Then he stopped and addressed Scrape who had been following enthusiastically. 'You don't come then. I talk to her alone. Just me and her.'

The little man stroked his beard thoughtfully. 'A good idea,' he said finally. 'A good idea. They will want an independent trial. They might think I am signalling her. A good thought, boy. But I will be close by. I will be in here, in the library. She calls it the toilet,' he added gleefully. Then he burst into a sleazy cackle.

Ralph gave him a look of disgust and then turned and pushed into the kitchen.

Linda turned round from where she was washing the dishes and took several steps backwards. Her face was even paler than before. Ralph understood now that she was frightened of him. Finally, however, she summoned up her courage and stepped forward, holding out her hand. 'Goodbye,' she said in a shaking voice.

'Goodbye?' queried Ralph. 'You want me to go?'

'Yes,' she said, shaking her head as she spoke.

Ralph took her outstretched hand and shook it. It was not a hand shake that said goodbye. It was warm and welcoming.

'Is this really the first time you have been alone with another person other than him?' asked Ralph, nodding towards the library.

'Don't call him a person,' she said with a hint of annoyance. 'We don't let persons in the laundry. Only animals are allowed here. The cats have kennels in the river.'

'You've got everything back to front,' said Ralph incredulously. 'All your words are mixed up.'

'Front to back,' she corrected, staring at him with a puzzled face. 'And you are the one with everything mixed down. You talk strangely. Are you drunk? I have heard that women behave strangely when they are drunk.'

Ralph's head began to spin. He couldn't take it all in. He didn't trust himself to speak. He remembered Dr Scrape's words, 'Dog is cat, tree is lamp post, ant is elephant, and just for fun, boy is girl.' Linda was looking at him as if he was mad. He walked over to the sink and picked up a fork. 'What's this?' he said, waving it around excitedly.

'A chicken of course,' she answered. Ralph could see by her look that she thought he was the one with the crazy speech.

'And what lays eggs and goes cluck, cluck?' He flapped his arms like wings as he said it.

The girl smiled with amusement. 'A fork. Haven't you ever seen a fork scratching for bananas?'

Ralph hung his head in his hands. 'Oh no,' he groaned. 'The swine has really mucked you up. You have got everything back to front – front to back. They don't dig for bananas. They dig for worms.' He stared at her with pity-filled eyes. She was completely confused. She was also the most beautiful girl he had ever seen. He bit his knuckles and thought over the situation carefully. 'Man' was 'woman'. 'Boy' was 'girl'. 'Ceiling' was 'floor'. But some words were right. 45

'Him' and 'her' were both correct. Suddenly he turned and ran from the room. He returned a second later holding Dr Scrape's exercise book. He flicked wildly through the pages, groaning and shaking his head as he read.

The girl looked frightened. She held her head up like a deer sniffing the wind. 'That glass must not be read,' she whispered, looking nervously towards the library. 'None of the glasses in the toilet can be read either.'

He ignored her fear. 'Now,' he said to himself. 'Let's try again.' He held the exercise book open in one hand for reference. Then he said slowly, 'Have you ever spoken to a girl like me before?'

'Yes,' said Linda shaking her head.

Ralph sighed and then tried again. He held up the fork. 'Is this a chicken?'

'No,' she said nodding her head. Ralph could see that she was regarding him with a mixture of fear, amusement and, yes, he would say, affection. Despite her bewilderment over what she considered to be his strange speech, she liked him.

Suddenly the enormity of the crime that had been

worked on this girl overwhelmed Ralph. He was filled with anger and pity. And disgust with Dr Scrape. Linda had never been to school. Never spoken to another person. Never been to the movies or a disco. For fourteen years she had spoken only to that monster Scrape. She had been a prisoner in this house. She had never been touched by another person . . . never been kissed.

There eyes met for an instant but the exchange was put to flight by the sound of coughing coming from the library.

'Quick,' said Ralph. 'There isn't much time. I want you to nod for "yes" and shake your head for "no" – drat, I mean the other way around.' He consulted the exercise book. 'I mean nod your head for "no" and shake your head for "yes".' He looked again at the book. The words were alphabetically listed. He couldn't be sure that she understood. What if the word for head was foot? Or the word for shake was dance, or something worse?

Linda paused and then nodded.

He tried again. 'Have you ever spoken to another animal except him?' he said jerking a contemptuous thumb in the direction of the library.

She shook her head sadly. It was true then. Scrape's story was true.

'Would you like to?' he asked slowly after finding that 'like' was not listed in the book.

She paused, looked a little fearful, and then keeping her eyes on his, nodded her head slowly.

'Tonight,' he whispered, and then, checking the book, 'No, today. At midnight, no sorry, midday. I will meet you. By that lamp post.' He pointed out of the window and across the rolling lawns of the mansion. 'By that lamp post. Do you understand?'

Linda followed his gaze. There was a lamp post at the far end of the driveway which could just be seen through the leaves of a large gum tree in the middle of the lawn. He took her hand. It was warm and soft and sent a current of happiness up his arm. He asked her again in a whisper. 'Do you understand?'

She nodded and for the first time he noticed a sparkle in her eyes.

'I didn't ask you to maul my son,' a voice hissed from behind them. Ralph jumped as a grip of steel took hold of his arm. Dr Scrape was incredibly strong.

He dragged Ralph out of the kitchen and into the

lounge. 'You stay in the laundry,' he snarled at Linda as the kitchen door swung closed in her face.

'Well, my boy,' he said with a twisted grin. 'How did it go? Could you make head or tail of what she said? Or should I say tail or head?' He licked his greasy moustache with satisfaction at his little joke.

Ralph tried to disguise the contempt he felt. 'What would happen if she mixed with people in the real world?' he asked. 'If she was to leave here and go to school? Would she learn to talk normally?'

Dr Scrape paused and looked carefully at Ralph as if reading his mind. 'Yes,' he said. 'Of course she would. She would model on the others. She would soon speak just like you I suspect. But that's not going to happen, is it?'

Ralph could contain himself no longer. 'You devil,' he yelled. 'You've mucked her up all right. She thinks I am the one who can't talk properly. She thinks I'm a bit crazy. But don't think I'm going to help you. I'll do everything I can to stop you. You're nothing but a vicious, crazy little monster.' He stood up and stormed out of the house.

49

Dr Scrape gave a wicked smile of satisfaction as Ralph disappeared down the long driveway.

It was thirty minutes past midnight and a few stars appeared occasionally when the drifting clouds allowed them to penetrate.

It was a different Ralph who stood waiting beneath the lamp post. Gone were the overalls, work boots and the smudged face. He wore his best jeans and his hair shone in the light of the street light. He had taken a lot of time over his appearance.

He looked anxiously at his watch and then up at the dark house. There was no sign of Linda. She was thirty minutes late. His heart sank as slowly and surely as the sun had done that evening. She wasn't coming. She had dismissed him as a funny-speaking crank. Or that evil man had guessed their plan and locked her in a room.

It began to drizzle and soon trickles of water ran down his neck. One o'clock and still no sign of her. He sighed and decided to go. There was nothing more he could do. She wasn't going to show up. The words started to keep time with his feet as he crunched homewards along the gravel road. 'Show up, show up'. Linda would have said 'show down' not 'show up.'

A bell rang in the back of his mind. A tiny, insistent bell of alarm. Once again he heard Dr Scrape speaking. 'Dog is cat, tree is lamp post, ant is . . .' Of course.

'Tree is lamp post. And therefore . . . lamp post is tree.' He almost shouted the words out. She called a lamp post a tree. Linda might have been waiting beneath the gum tree in the middle of the gardens while he was waiting under the lamp post by the gate. He hardly dared hope. He ran blindly in the dark night. Several times he fell over. Once he put a hole in the knee of his jeans but he didn't give it a thought.

He knew that she would have gone. Like him she would have given up waiting and have returned to the dark house.

At last he stumbled up to the tree, finding it by its silhouette against the black sky. 'Linda,' he whispered urgently, using her name for the first time. It tasted sweet on his lips.

There was no answer.

Then, at the foot of the house, in the distance, he saw a flicker of yellow light. It looked like a candle. 51

He saw Linda, faintly, holding the small flame. Before he could call out she opened the front door and disappeared inside.

'Damn and blast,' he said aloud. He smashed his clenched fist into the trunk of the tree in disappointment. A lump of bitter anguish welled up in his throat. He threw himself heavily down on the damp ground to wait. Perhaps she would try again. Anyway, he resolved to stay there until morning.

Inside the dark house Linda made her way back to her bedroom upstairs. Her eyes were wet with tears of rejection. The strange girl had not come. She crept silently, terrified of awaking her tormentor. Holding the forbidden candle in her left hand she tiptoed up the stairs. She held her breath as she reached the landing lest her guardian should feel its gentle breeze even from behind closed doors.

'Betrayed, betrayed,' shrieked a figure from the darkness. The candle was struck from her hand and spiralled over the handrail to the floor below. It spluttered dimly in the depths.

The dark form of Dr Scrape began slapping Linda's frail cheeks. Over and over he slapped, accompanying every blow with same shrill word. 'Betrayed, betrayed, betrayed.'

In fear, in shock, in desperation, the girl pushed at the flaying shadow. Losing his footing, Scrape tumbled backwards, over and over, down the wooden staircase. He came to a halt halfway down and lay still.

Linda collapsed on to the top step, sobbing into her hands, not noticing the smoke swirling up from below. Then, awakened to her peril by the crackling flames that raced up the stairs, she filled her lungs with smoke-filled air, screamed and fainted dead away.

The old mansion was soon burning like a house of straws. Flames leapt from the windows and leaked from the tiles. Smoke danced before the moonless sky.

The roar of falling timber awakened Ralph from a fitful doze at the base of the tree. He ran, blindly, wildly, unthinkingly through the blazing front door and through the swirling smoke, made out Linda's crumpled form at the top of the staircase. He ran to her, jumping three steps at a time, ignoring the scorching flames and not feeling the licking pain on his legs. Staggering, grunting, breathing smoke he struggled with her limp body past the unconscious form of Dr

Scrape. He paused, and saw in that second that Scrape was still breathing and that his eyes were wide and staring. He seemed unable to move. Ralph charged past him, forward, through the burning door and along the winding driveway. Only the sight of an ambulance and fire truck allowed him to let go and fall with his precious load, unconscious on the wet grass.

'Smoke inhalation,' yelled the ambulance driver. 'Get oxygen and put them both in the back.'

Linda's eyes flickered open and she stared in awe from the stretcher at the uniformed figure. Only the third person she had seen in her life. A mask was lowered over her face, but not before she had time to notice that the unconscious Ralph was breathing quietly on the stretcher next to her.

'I want to speak to her,' yelled the fire chief striding over from the flashing truck.

'No way, they are both going to hospital,' shouted the ambulance driver in answer.

The fire chief ignored the reply and tore the mask from Linda's gasping mouth. He bent close to her. 'I can't send men in there,' he yelled, pointing at the blazing house. 'Not unless there is someone inside. Is there anyone inside?'

'Mother,' whispered the girl.

The fireman looked around. 'She said mother.'

'She hasn't got a mother,' said a short bald man who had come over from the house next door. 'Her mother died when the girl was born. She only has a father. Dr Scrape.'

The fireman leaned closer. His words were urgent. 'Is your father in there, girl? Is anyone in there? The roof is about to collapse. Is anyone inside the house?'

Linda tried to make sense of his strange speech. Then a look of enlightenment swept across her face. She understood the question — that was clear. But many have wondered if she understood her own answer.

As the ambulance driver shut the door she just had time to say one word.

'No.'

Penguin Children's 60s